**WARNING!**

SCAREDY SQUIRREL ASKS
EVERYONE TO COVER THEIR
NOSES TO AVOID FROSTBITE.

# THE HOLIDAY

**1. CHRISTMASTIME MAKES ME...**

GRUMPY ☐ (0 points)

FESTIVE ☐ (1 point)

PANICKY ☐ (1 point)

**2. THIS YEAR I WAS...**

NAUGHTY ☐ (0 points)

NICE ☐ (1 point)

GARY (THE GERM) ☐ (−87 points)

**3. SEEING MISTLETOE MAKES ME...**

HAPPY ☐ (0 points)

PUT ON CHAPSTICK ☐ (0 points)

NERVOUS ☐ (1 point)

**4. DASHING THROUGH THE SNOW...**

IN A ONE-HORSE OPEN SLEIGH ☐ (0 points)

SOUNDS DANGEROUS ☐ (1 point)

# READER QUIZ

**5.** MY TREE MUST BE...

REAL ☐ (0 points)

FAKE ☐ (0 points)

TERMITE-FREE ☐ (1 point)

**6.** A JACK-IN-THE-BOX MAKES...

A GREAT GIFT ☐ (0 points)

A NICE SURPRISE ☐ (0 points)

ME JUMP 8 FEET UP IN THE AIR! ☐ (1 point)

**7.** ON THE FIRST DAY OF CHRISTMAS, MY TRUE LOVE GAVE TO ME...

A PARTRIDGE IN A PEAR TREE ☐ (0 points)

HAND SANITIZER ☐ (1 point)

**8.** WHAT DO YOU SEE?

RUDOLPH THE RED-NOSED REINDEER ☐ (0 points)

AN UNIDENTIFIED FLYING OBJECT FROM OUTER SPACE WITH ANTENNAE AND AN ALARMING TRACKING DEVICE! ☐ (3 points)

CONGRATULATIONS!
IF YOUR TOTAL POINTS ARE BETWEEN 1 AND 10,
YOU CAN SAFELY PROCEED TO THE NEXT PAGE.

# Scaredy Squirrel

## Gets Festive

## BY MELANIE WATT

tundra

# FOR VICTORIA, GINA AND JONATHAN

Copyright © 2023 by Melanie Watt

Tundra Books, an imprint of Tundra Book Group,
a division of Penguin Random House of Canada Limited

Library and Archives Canada Cataloguing in Publication

Title: Scaredy Squirrel gets festive / Melanie Watt.
Names: Watt, Mélanie, 1975- author, illustrator.
Series: Watt, Mélanie, 1975- Scaredy's nutty adventures ; 3.
Description: Series statement: Scaredy's nutty adventures; 3
Identifiers: Canadiana (print) 20220437823 | Canadiana (ebook) 20220437831 | ISBN 9780735269613 (hardcover) | ISBN 9780735269620 (EPUB)
Classification: LCC PS8645.A884 S2828 2023 | DDC jC813/.6—dc23

Edited by Tara Walker and Michelle Nagler
Designed by Melanie Watt
The artwork in this book was rendered in charcoal pencil and colored digitally in Photoshop.
The text was set in Garden Gnome.

Printed in China

www.penguinrandomhouse.ca

1  2  3  4  5      27  26  25  24  23

Penguin
Random House
TUNDRA BOOKS

# MERRY CONTENTS

# CHAPTER 1
## PICTURE PERFECT

SCAREDY SQUIRREL
STARTS PREPARING
FOR CHRISTMAS...

... IN JULY.

HE MAKES A LIST AND CHECKS
IT WAY MORE THAN TWICE.

# Scaredy's Christmas TO-DO List:

- [ ] Install PERFECT red and green decorations
- [ ] Guarantee PERFECT safety
- [ ] Build PERFECT gingerbread house
- [ ] Wrap PERFECT gifts
- [ ] Throw PERFECT get-together
- [ ] Set up PERFECT spot for Santa Claus
- [ ] Watch the PERFECT snowfall on Christmas morning

NOW THAT IT'S DECEMBER, SCAREDY CAN FINALLY START CHECKING ITEMS OFF HIS LIST. EVERYTHING MUST BE PERFECT!

SOUNDS LIKE IT'S TIME TO DECORATE!

NO...
IT'S ME, IVY!
I'M WEARING A
CUTE REINDEER
HEADBAND!

OOPS!
HELLO, IVY!

AND WHAT
ON EARTH IS
A JACKALOPE?

jack·a·lope
*mythical creature*
(73% jackrabbit / 27% antelope)

WOW.
IT'S LIKE
LOOKING
IN A
MIRROR.

15

YODEL-AY-HEE-HOO!! TIM!! RASH!!

22

OBVIOUSLY, THIS KETCHUP MATCHES YOUR RED!

YES, BUT IT'S NOT VERY CHRISTMASSY.

WAS THAT IN RASH'S BIN?

FOR A SPLASH OF GREEN, I NOMINATE CHUCKY, MY PET TOAD!

THERE WAS A **LIVE** CRITTER IN THERE TOO?

RELAX! HE'S POTTY-TRAINED!

| NO RED: | NO GREEN: |
|---|---|

CHILI PEPPERS     STREET SIGNS     MARTIANS     POISON IVY

ANTS     FIRECRACKERS     BUGS

FIRE HYDRANTS     POISON BERRIES     GODZILLA     CACTI

WELL...**THAT** RULES OUT E-V-E-R-Y-THING!

SO LET'S GET CREATIVE! LOOK WHAT I'VE FOUND...

OLD PING-PONG BALLS

UH, THOSE ARE **VINTAGE.**

THEN IT'S SETTLED! WE'RE HAVING A PING-PONG TOURNAMENT!

CLOSE, BUT NO.

WE'RE MAKING ORNAMENTS!

[sound of crickets hibernating]

BY PAINTING THE PING-PONG BALLS RED AND GREEN, WE'LL HAVE PERFECT DECORATIONS!

OH-H-H! GREAT IDEA!

YEAH! PAINTER'S SUITS FOR EVERYONE!

LET'S DO THIS!

THEY MIX THE COLORS...

PAINT SOME
PING-PONG BALLS RED...

PAINT THE OTHERS GREEN...

AND DECORATE!

# CHAPTER 2
## HOLIDAY TROUBLE

SCAREDY SQUIRREL
MUST SECURE THE AREA
BEFORE CHRISTMAS.

WAIT A MINUTE! YOU NEED TO DO WHAT?

KEEP THE HOLIDAY TROUBLEMAKERS AWAY!

IS THIS ABOUT THAT JACKALOPE AGAIN?

UH, DON'T FORGET...

TOOTHY NUTCRACKERS

ABOMINABLE SNOWMEN

# ELVES

POINTY HAT

POINTY EYEBROWS

POINTY TOY-MAKING POWER DRILL

POINTY EARS

WHOPPING AMOUNT OF STINKY PEPPERMINT COLOGNE

POINTY SHOES

SCAREDY, YOU HAD ME AT PEPPERMINT!

YOU HAD ME AT POWER DRILL!

LET'S SECURE THIS PLACE!

NOW THAT'S THE HOLIDAY SPIRIT!

SCAREDY, TIM, RASH AND IVY SAFEGUARD THE AREA.

REFLECTIVE TRAFFIC CONES

NO TROUBLEMAKERS SIGN

PERFECT!

# CHAPTER 3
## GINGERBREAD PLAN

SCAREDY SQUIRREL
HAS BEEN BUSY WITH
HIS HOLIDAY BAKING.

37

HO! HO! NO. WE'RE NOT MAKING A GINGERBREAD HOUSE WE CAN EAT!

LA! LA! LA! I'M NOT LISTENING!

CHRISTMAS IS RUINED!!

UH... WHAT KIND OF HOUSE ARE WE MAKING, THEN?

THE KIND WE CAN FEAST OUR EYES ON!!

BUT EYEBALLS CAN'T CHEW!

FA! LA! LA! LA!

IF WE DON'T EAT THE HOUSE, WE CAN KEEP IT FOR-EV-ER!

SERIOUSLY? I DOUBT GINGERBREAD CAN LAST PAST EASTER.

YULE LOG

C'MON, TEAM!
LET'S BUILD A HOUSE THAT
WILL LAST FOR DECADES!

I HOPE IT WON'T TAKE THAT LONG TO FIND CHUCKY.

# GINGERBREAD CONSTRUCTION MATERIALS:

GLUE

MARBLES

VARNISH

FAN

# STEP 1: ASSEMBLE THE WALLS AND ROOF

# STEP 2: DECORATE THE HOUSE WITH GLUE AND MARBLES

**STEP 3:** APPLY GLOSSY VARNISH ALL OVER THE HOUSE

**STEP 4:** LET DRY FOR 3 HOURS AND 24 MINUTES

# CHAPTER 4
## GIFT GIVING 101

SCAREDY SQUIRREL
KNOWS HOW TO PICK OUT
THE PERFECT HOLIDAY GIFTS.

**NAME:** IVY

**PERSONALITY:** BRAINY TYPE

**LIKES:** READING A TON

**DISLIKES:** SHORT BOOKS

**PERFECT GIFT:** FESTIVE NOVEL

**NAME:** RASH

**PERSONALITY:** GUTSY TYPE

**LIKES:** THRILLS, LOOKING COOL

**DISLIKES:** BEIGE

**PERFECT GIFT:** 3D GLASSES

**NAME:** TIM

**PERSONALITY:** HUNGRY TYPE

**LIKES:** EATING

**DISLIKES:** NOT EATING

**PERFECT GIFT:** SNACK

WOOD CHIPS

BBQ & MAPLE FLAVOR

AND IS EAGER TO
WRAP THINGS UP!

49

# HOW TO WRAP THE PERFECT GIFT

## PUT ON CRAFTING GEAR:

SHOWER CAP KEEPS FUR IN PLACE

GOGGLES BLOCK RUNAWAY GLITTER

GLOVES PREVENT PAPER CUTS

APRON GIVES FESTIVE LOOK

## MAKE SURE TO WRAP OUT OF SIGHT:

# CHOOSE A NICE PACKAGE:

## STOCKING
PROS: FAST AND EASY!
CONS: MIGHT SMELL LIKE FEET

## PAPER BAG
PROS: FAST AND EASY!
CONS: ITEMS COULD FALL OUT

## ☑ BOX
PROS: FUN AND EASY TO UNWRAP!
CONS: NONE. IT'S PERFECT!

# GATHER THE RIGHT TOOLS:

**2 MEASURING TAPES**
(TO MEASURE TWICE)

**SAFETY SCISSORS**

**INVISIBLE TAPE**

**WRAPPING PAPER**

**RIBBON**

SCAREDY MUST BE WRAPPING CHRISTMAS PRESENTS!!!

AWW! WHAT SHOULD WE GET SCAREDY? OH, I KNOW! ONE OF THOSE FANCY . . .

FRUIT BOUQUETS

2 WORDS: FRUIT FLIES.

SCAREDY WOULD MUCH RATHER GET A PAIR OF SOLAR-POWERED . . .

ROLLER SKATES

3 WORDS: LET'S KEEP THINKING.

OUR FRIEND DESERVES A SPECIAL GIFT! SOMETHING HE WON'T BE EXPECTING!

WHAT FRIEND?

OH, LOOK! SCAREDY HAS RETURNED.

MAYBE I CAN HELP YOU PICK OUT A GIFT FOR THIS FRIEND OF YOURS?

UH, SURE. THAT'S NOT AWKWARD AT ALL!

UNLESS THIS FRIEND IS...

ALRIGHTY! HOW WOULD YOU DESCRIBE THIS FRIEND?

- FUNNY TYPE?
- GRUMPY TYPE?
- SPORTY TYPE?
- OUTDOORSY TYPE?
- MUSICAL TYPE?
- SERIOUS TYPE?
- EASYGOING TYPE?

DEFINITELY NOT THAT LAST ONE!

I'D SAY HE'S A MINDFUL, PRUDENT, REMARKABLY ALERT, GOOD-NATURED, ASTONISHINGLY ORGANIZED TYPE.

AND OUTDOORSY, IF MOSQUITOES AREN'T AROUND.

HMM...

THEN I'D PLAY IT SAFE AND GO WITH A GIFT CARD.

4 WORDS: UH, LET'S KEEP THINKING.

# CHAPTER 5
## THE NON-PARTY

SCAREDY SQUIRREL AND
HIS FRIENDS ARE PREPARING
THEIR CHRISTMAS EVE
GET-TOGETHER.

I WOULDN'T CALL IT A PARTY. JUST A QUIET, CASUAL GET-TOGETHER!

CASUAL? BUT YOU HANDED OUT INVITATIONS MONTHS AGO!

SCAREDY INVITES YOU: TIM DECEMBER 24TH

SCAREDY INVITES YOU: RASH DECEMBER 24TH

SCAREDY INVITES YOU: IVY DECEMBER 24TH

*FLASHBACK TO JULY*

AND LOOKEE HERE, I'VE FOUND A DEFINITION...

**PAR·TY** (noun)
a gathering of invited guests, involving food
(like carrot cupcakes)
and music

WE'RE GONNA HAVE YUMMY TACOS, RIGHT, SCAREDY?

... AND A CHOCOLATE FOUNTAIN? AND MUSIC?

SOUNDS LOUD AND MESSY!

I'LL BRING EXTRA PARTY NAPKINS!

OR WE COULD HAVE...

61

A TEA PARTY!

'TIS A MARVELOUS IDEA!
SIMPLY DELIGHTFUL!
A LOVELY PARTY INDEED!
BAH! HUMBUG! WHY AM I THE ONLY ONE WHO CAN'T LIFT UP MY PINKIE?
HAND SANITIZER
PICTURE IT!
SOFT CLARINET MUSIC, TINY TEA SANDWICHES AND CHESTNUTS NOT ROASTING ON AN OPEN FIRE.

63

65

# FAKE FIREPLACE

ONE BY ONE, THE FRIENDS HANG THEIR CHRISTMAS STOCKINGS.

SCAREDY, IVY, TIM AND RASH START THEIR HOLIDAY FEAST.

THEY ENJOY THE CHOCOLATE FOUNTAIN UNTIL...

AND CLEAN UP FOR 57 MINUTES.

## THEY PLAY PARTY GAMES...

## SING HOLIDAY SONGS...

# SANTA CLAUS

MAKES THE BEST, LONGEST LISTS IN THE UNIVERSE

WEARS GLOVES TO BLOCK GERMS

NICE:

Scaredy

Ivy

Tim

Rash

Easter Bunny

Tooth Fairy

NAUGHTY:

Gary the Germ

Toothy Nutcrackers

Abominable Snowmen

Jack Frost

Frostbiters

Pointy Elves

73

SCAREDY, IVY, TIM AND RASH ADMIRE THEIR PERFECT SETUP...

AND HURRY TO BED WITH VISIONS OF CHRISTMAS
DANCING IN THEIR HEADS.

# CHAPTER 6
## CHRISTMAS MORNING

SCAREDY SQUIRREL AND HIS FRIENDS WAKE UP TO AN AMAZING SIGHT.

YIPPEE! SANTA LEFT GIFTS IN OUR STOCKINGS!

AND HALF OF A COOKIE!

SCAREDY SQUIRREL PANICS AND PLAYS DEAD.

2 HOURS LATER...

EVERYONE LOOKS INSIDE THEIR STOCKINGS. SANTA HAS BROUGHT THEM ALL...

NOW SCAREDY HANDS OUT HIS PRESENTS.

AWW! I LOVE IT!

BEST GIFT EVER!

I'M SPEECHLESS, SCAREDY!

A CHRISTMAS CAROL

WOOD CHIPS

AH, NUTS! THE ONLY THING WE CAN'T CHECK OFF MY LIST IS THE PERFECT SNOWFALL.

YUP, 'CAUSE CONTROLLING THE WEATHER IS, UH... IMPOSSIBLE!

I SHOULD ASK SANTA FOR A SNOWMAKING MACHINE NEXT YEAR.

SNOW GLOBE →

Scaredy's Christmas
TO-DO list:

- ☑ Install PERFECT red and green decorations
- ☑ Guarantee PERFECT
- ☑ Build PERFECT gingerbread house
- ☑ Wrap PERFECT gifts
- ☑ Throw PERFECT get-together
- ☑ Set up PERFECT spot for Santa Claus
- ☑ Watch the PERFECT snowfall on Christmas morning . . . with friends!

THE END

# FAQ

(FREQUENTLY ASKED QUESTIONS)

**Q1** SCAREDY, WILL YOU BE BACK WITH NEW NUTTY ADVENTURES?

**S.O.S.:** YES! I have to face my fears of banana peels, falling coconuts and leprechauns.

GOOD LUCK, ME SQUIRREL!

**Q2** SCAREDY, WHAT DOES THE "O" IN YOUR INITIALS STAND FOR?

**S.O.S.:** My middle name is Orville, after the famous Orville Wright, who was the first to fly a plane.

**Q3** WHAT WOULD BE YOUR WORST-CASE SCENARIO DURING CHRISTMAS?

**S.O.S.:** Easy! Coming face-to-face with Gary the germ, standing under the mistletoe.

**Q4** SCAREDY, WHAT'S THE BEST HOLIDAY ADVICE YOU CAN GIVE?

**S.O.S.:** Always measure twice before you start cutting Christmas wrapping paper.

**Q5** SCAREDY, WHAT ARE YOUR PICTURE BOOK TITLES?

AND MY NUTTY GRAPHIC NOVELS!

**S.O.S.:**
- Scaredy Squirrel
- Scaredy Squirrel Makes a Friend
- Scaredy Squirrel at the Beach
- Scaredy Squirrel at Night
- Scaredy Squirrel Has a Birthday Party
- Scaredy Squirrel Goes Camping
- Scaredy Squirrel Visits the Doctor